FATHER FIGURES

LARRY'S JOURNEY TO MANHOOD

WRITTEN BY
DERRICH PHILLIPS

ILLUSTRATED BY
JASMINE MILLS

Copyright © 2019 Mentor Select Publishing
Published 2020 by Mentor Select Publishing
Author Derrich Phillips
Illustrator Jasmine Mills
Editor Tracy Hundley
All rights reserved. No part of this publication may be reproduced, distributed, or transmitted in any form or by any means, including photocopying, recording, or other electronic or mechanical methods, without the prior written permission of the publisher, except in the case of brief quotations embodied in critical reviews and certain other noncommercial uses permitted by copyright law. Library of Congress Cataloging-in-Publication Data
ISBN: 978-1-950715-02-2
Printed in the United States of America
First Edition, February 2020
info@derrichphillips.com
www.father-figures.com

THIS BOOK BELONGS TO:

_____

_____

Larry loves adventure. He enjoys being outdoors swimming, fishing, and playing basketball with his friends.

Larry lives with his mother and older sister Tina. He lost his father at a very young age.

"Don't worry, Larry," his mom said when he told her his fears. "You'll learn everything you need to know to be a great man."

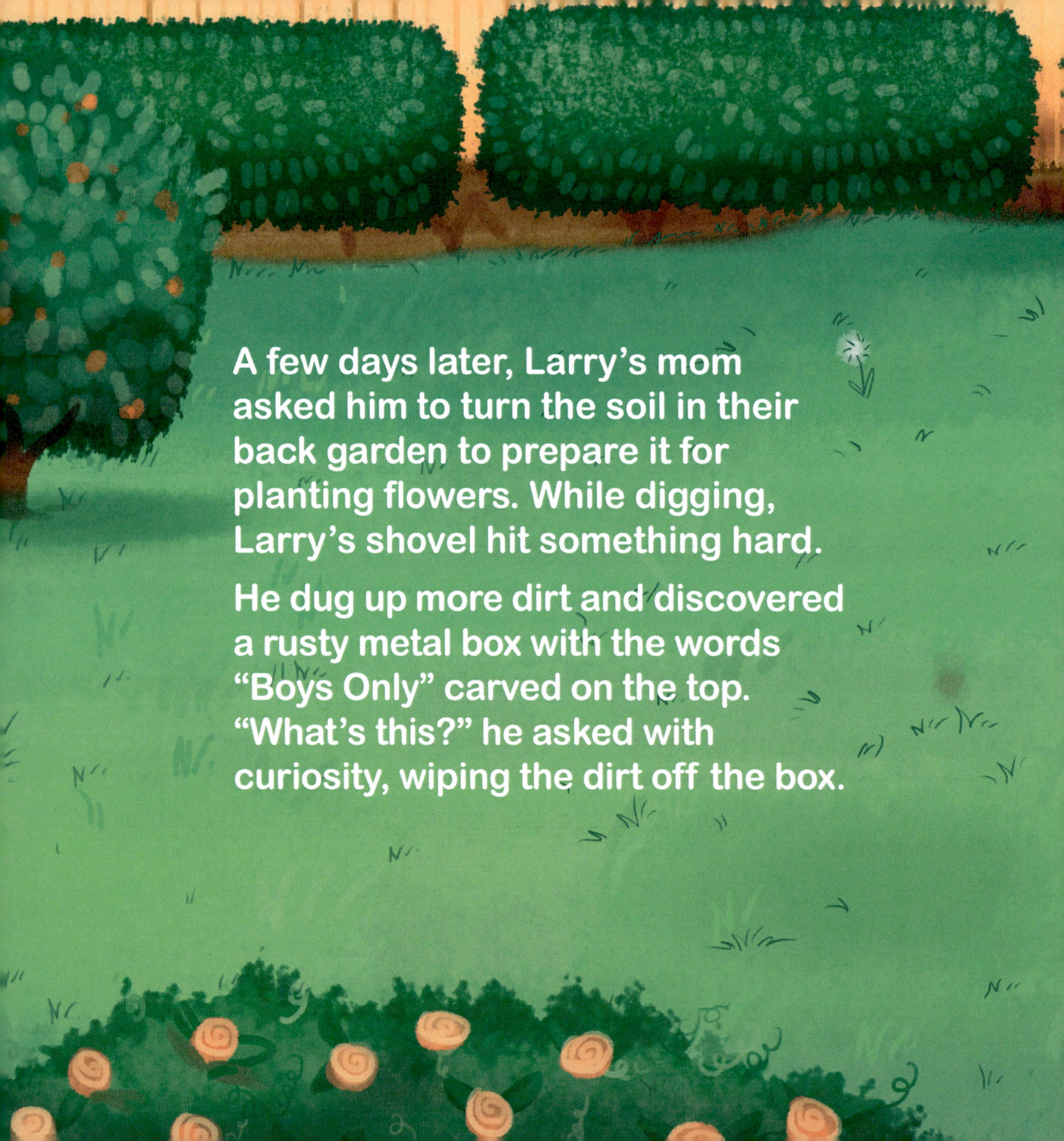

A few days later, Larry's mom asked him to turn the soil in their back garden to prepare it for planting flowers. While digging, Larry's shovel hit something hard.

He dug up more dirt and discovered a rusty metal box with the words "Boys Only" carved on the top. "What's this?" he asked with curiosity, wiping the dirt off the box.

Cautiously, he opened the metal box and saw a rolled-up piece of paper inside. The paper was wrinkled and tied with a piece of blue yarn.

Larry carefully picked it up, untied the yarn, and unrolled it. He saw hand-written words on the paper.

Larry read the words out loud: "Five qualities that a boy must possess to become a man."
His eyes widened and he became very excited as he continued reading:

1. Responsible
2. Disciplined
3. Humble
4. Brave
5. Honest

Excited to have a roadmap to manhood, Larry rushed back into the house to show his mom what he discovered.

"Mom, see what I found!" he shouted joyously as he handed her the paper.

His mom read the list and smiled.

"Mom, if I possess those qualities, will I become a man?" he asked, pointing at the paper.

"Yes, you sure will, Larry," his mom replied, smiling.

Larry frowned. "But how will I learn to possess those qualities?"

His mom patted his cheek. "Don't you worry, Larry. I know several men who have these qualities.

I'll find some who are willing to teach you how to be like them."

Larry couldn't stop grinning.

At the beginning of the summer, Larry's mom made a list of all the men she knew and respected.

Then, she considered each man's personality while looking at the five qualities on Larry's list.

For each quality, she selected one man who most consistently demonstrated that quality.

When Larry's mom finished narrowing down the names on her list, she contacted the men and informed them that Larry would like to shadow them for a day.

She explained what she had in mind. All the men whom she contacted happily agreed to be of help.

1. Responsible

Larry and his mom and sister were having dinner on a Sunday evening.

"Larry, Uncle Tommy will pick you up at 5:00 a.m. tomorrow," Larry's mom told him. "You are going to work with him to learn about being responsible."

Uncle Tommy was his mom's older brother. He was the hardest working man his mom knew. He worked at the local car factory.

Larry was so excited that he could barely sleep that night. His lessons on becoming a man would begin in the morning!

At exactly 5:00 a.m. on Monday morning, Uncle Tommy pulled into the driveway. Larry was already awake and ready to go.

Uncle Tommy drove to the car factory where he worked on an assembly line building cars.

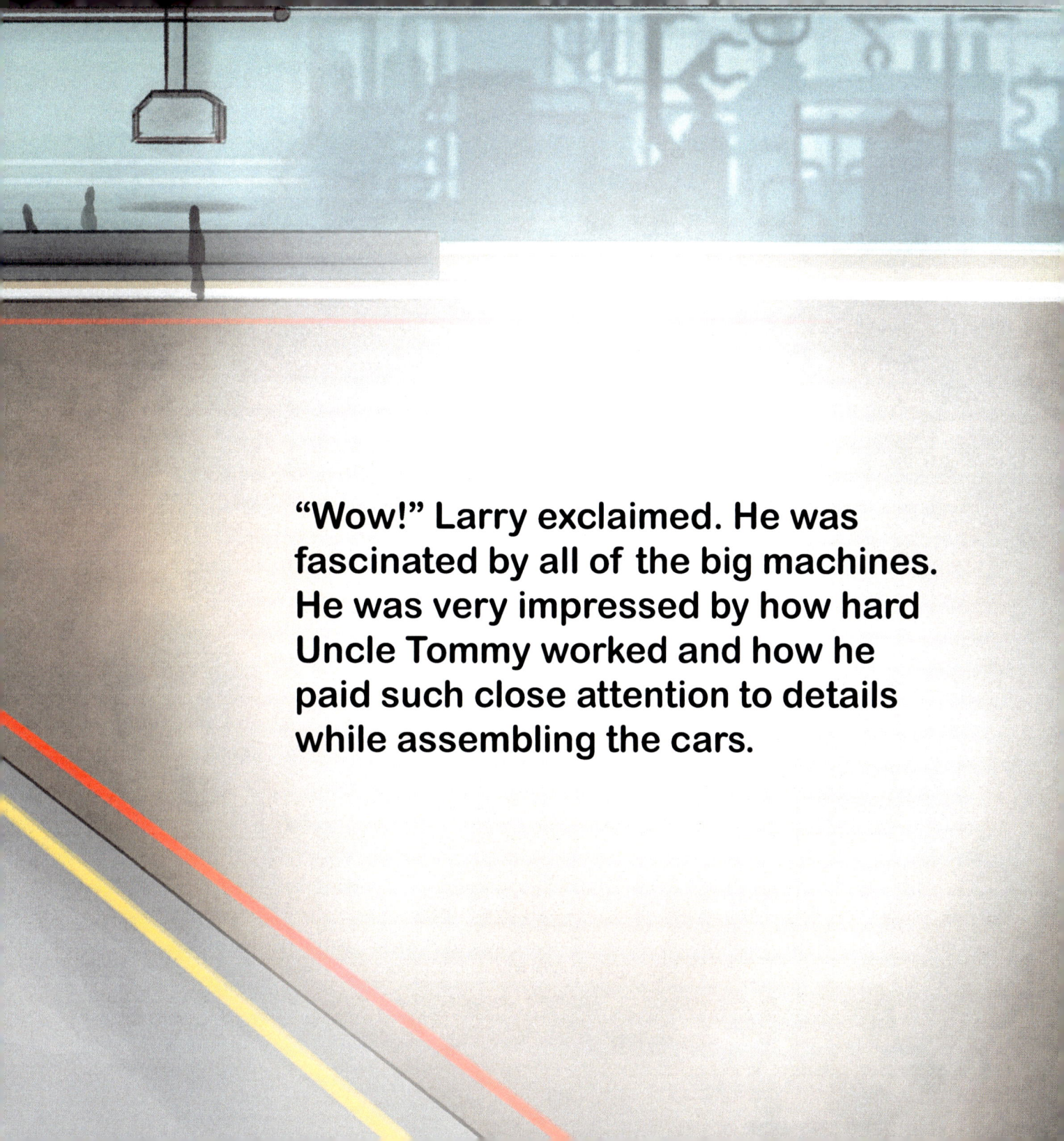

"Wow!" Larry exclaimed. He was fascinated by all of the big machines. He was very impressed by how hard Uncle Tommy worked and how he paid such close attention to details while assembling the cars.

"Larry, the man is the head of the home and has a lot of responsibilities. So, it's very important for men to work hard," his uncle told him at the close of work that day.

"As a man, you have to take pride in your work no matter what it is," he added. "You always have to go above and beyond to do the best job possible. Always give it your all."

Larry nodded.

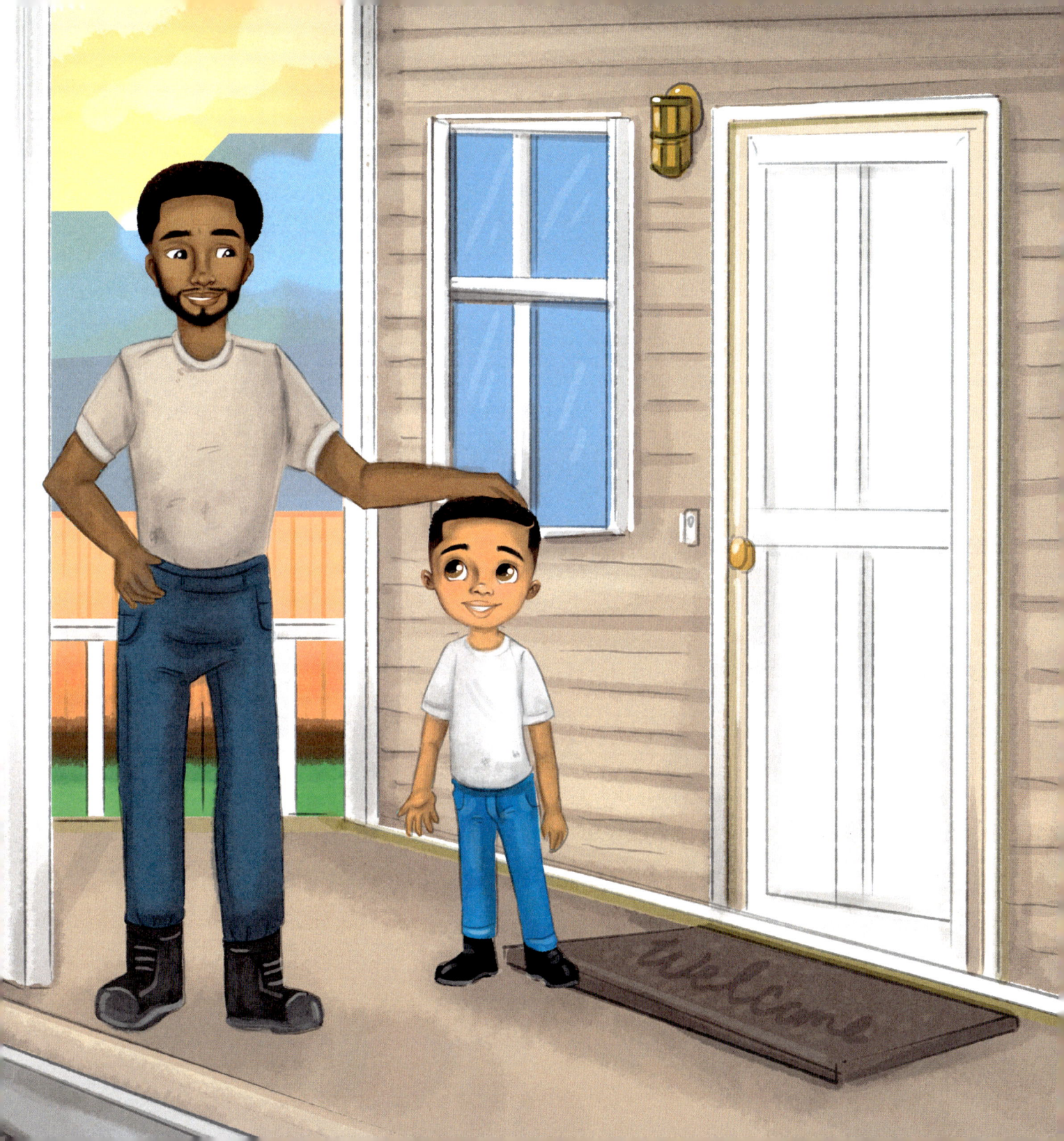

2. Disciplined

That night, Larry's mom said, "Larry, tomorrow you'll be visiting with Coach Jones. He's the high school track and field coach.

He coached your father when he was in high school, and he's the most disciplined man I know."

It was time for Larry to learn his next lesson.

"Okay, Mom," Larry said, eager to meet his dad's old coach.

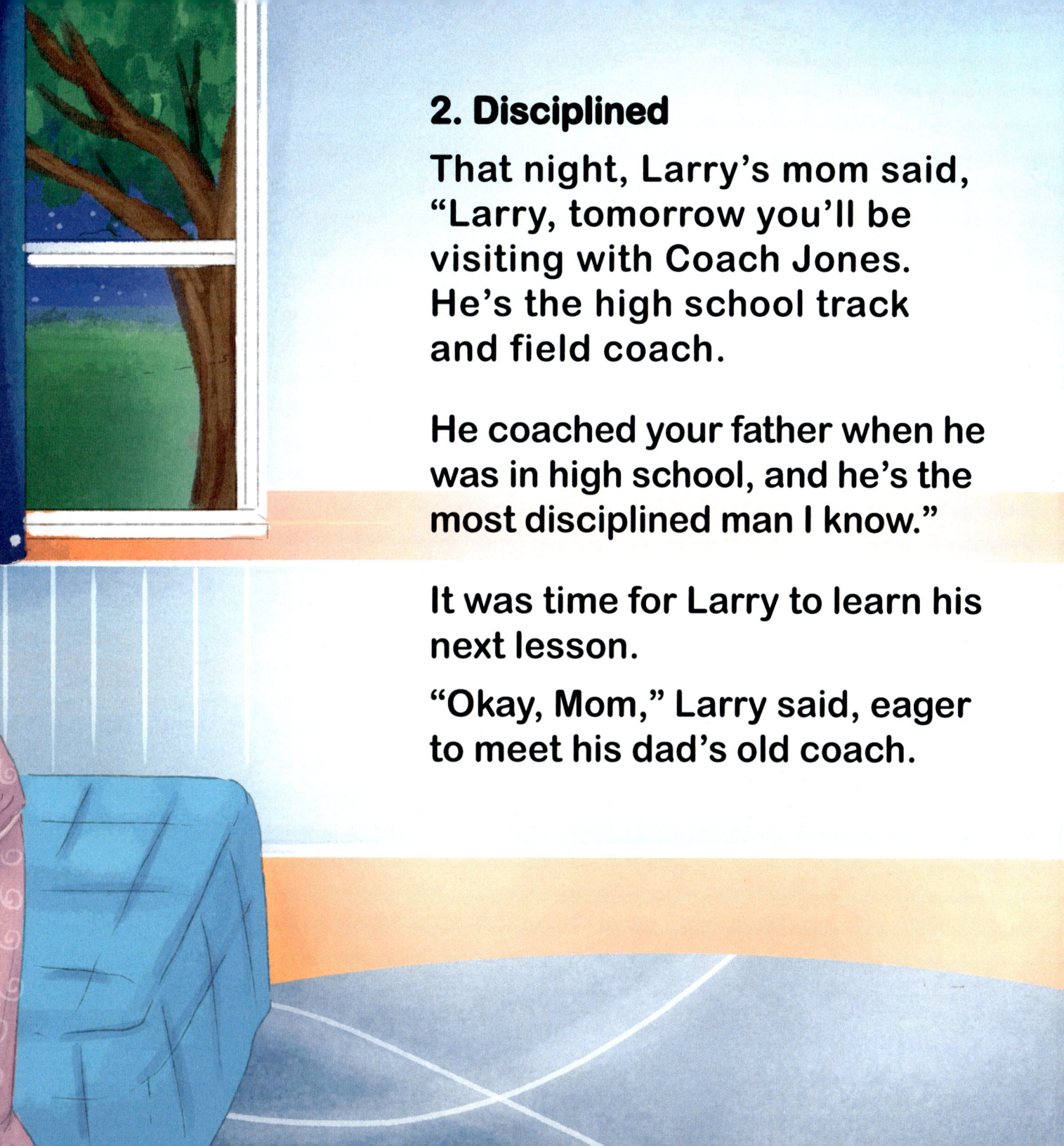

The following day, his mom took him to the school where Coach Jones was training the boys track team.

"Hello, Larry. Are you ready to learn about discipline?" the coach asked.

"Yes, Coach," Larry answered.

"Good. Now go run four laps around the track," Coach Jones said.

Larry was surprised, but he did as the man instructed. By the time he finished the second lap around the track, he was tired. He wanted to stop, but Coach Jones wouldn't let him.

"Oh, no, you don't, Larry. This is what it means to have discipline. You have to finish whatever you start.

You can't stop halfway simply because you're tired," the coach said firmly. "A man fights through discomfort and pain to cross the finish line at all costs.

Think about all the rights and freedoms that we enjoy in America today because our ancestors did not give up when they were tired and uncomfortable."

Motivated by Coach Jones' speech, Larry took a deep breath and began running again until he completed all four laps. He was dog-tired but proud that he had done it.

"Good job, Larry!" Coach Jones praised him, which made Larry even happier.

By the end of the workout, Larry had a greater understanding of what is required to be disciplined.

3. Humble

"Larry, you'll learn humility from a local businessman called Miguel," his mom told him one evening. "He owns several restaurants around town."

Larry was surprised when Miguel arrived at his house on a bike the following day.

"Hello, Larry. I'm Miguel," the businessman said and shook hands with Larry. "Let's go."

Larry followed Miguel to his restaurant on his own bike.

Throughout the day, Larry observed how Miguel went above and beyond to give his customers unforgettable dining experiences. He was always busy, but he took time to greet and talk to his customers, asking about their jobs and families.

Miguel dressed modestly. He did not wear anything that would make other people know he was rich. He treated his employees with respect. He didn't ask them to do any task that he wouldn't do himself. He took out the trash, cleaned the kitchen, and even cooked.

"Why do you ride a bicycle to work when you could buy a fancy car?" Larry asked Miguel at the end of the day. "And why are you so humble at your restaurant when you are the boss?"

Miguel smiled. "Even though I am financially successful now, I still remember what my dad taught me: always be humble regardless of your social status, and always treat people with respect.

Larry, remember to treat people better than you want to be treated, and you will live a happy, rich life."

4. Brave

The next day Larry's mother took Larry to the police station to learn bravery from a police officer named David. The man was a family friend who was eager to have Larry come to the station.

David was big and strong. He'd been a police officer for over ten years. He loved his job because he got to serve and protect the community.

Larry smiled when David gave him his police cap to wear. He beamed excitedly as he rode in David's police car with the sirens blaring.

While sitting in the patrol car, Larry watched as David chased a man who stole an old woman's purse. The lady was happy and grateful when her purse was returned with all its contents.

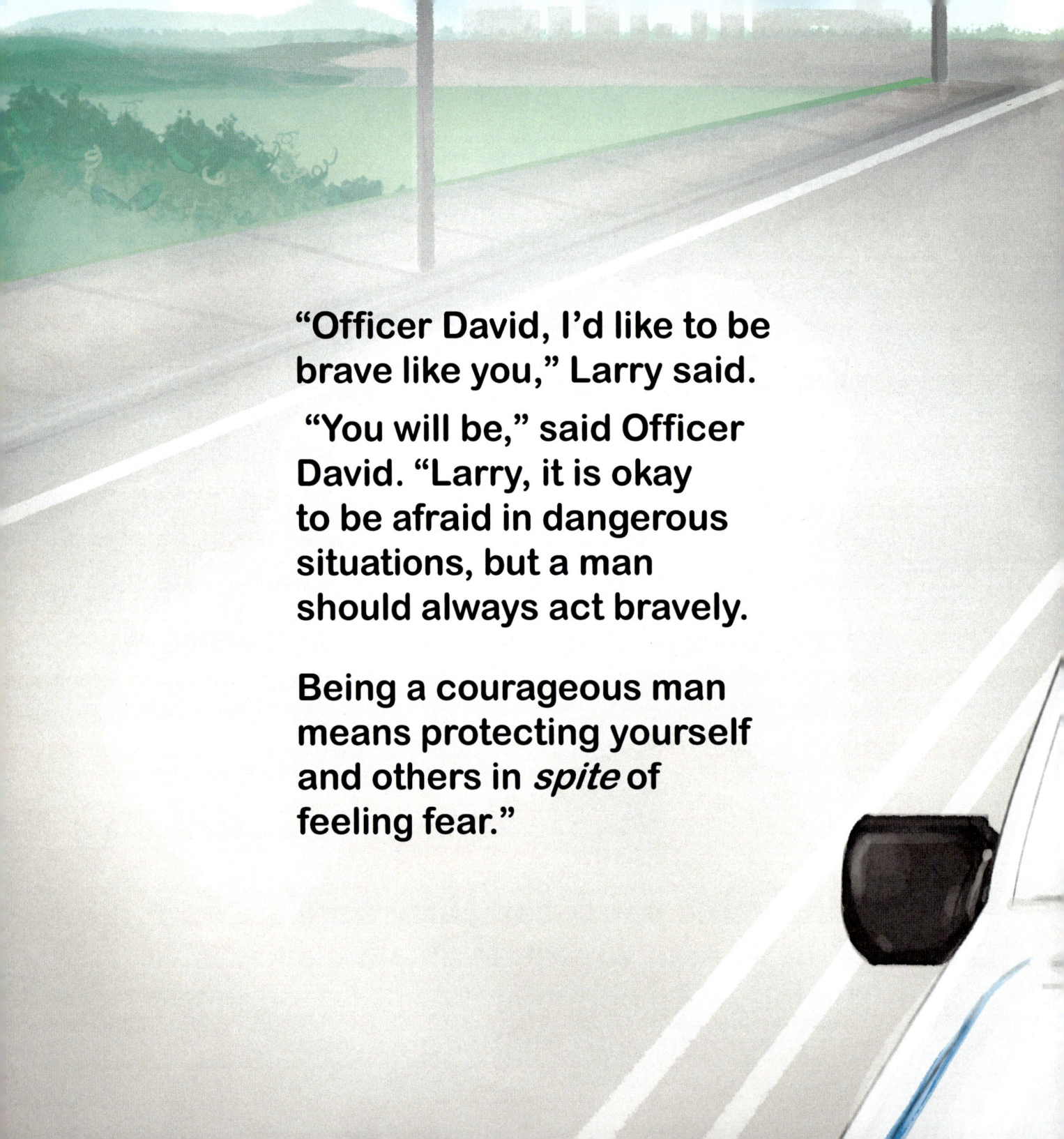

"Officer David, I'd like to be brave like you," Larry said.

"You will be," said Officer David. "Larry, it is okay to be afraid in dangerous situations, but a man should always act bravely.

Being a courageous man means protecting yourself and others in *spite* of feeling fear."

5. Honest

The next man Larry's mom introduced him to was the city mayor, Prince.

"I'm honored to meet you, Larry," Mayor Prince said to the small boy as he shook his hand.

Larry was delighted to be in the mayor's large office that day and eager to watch him as he took care of city business.

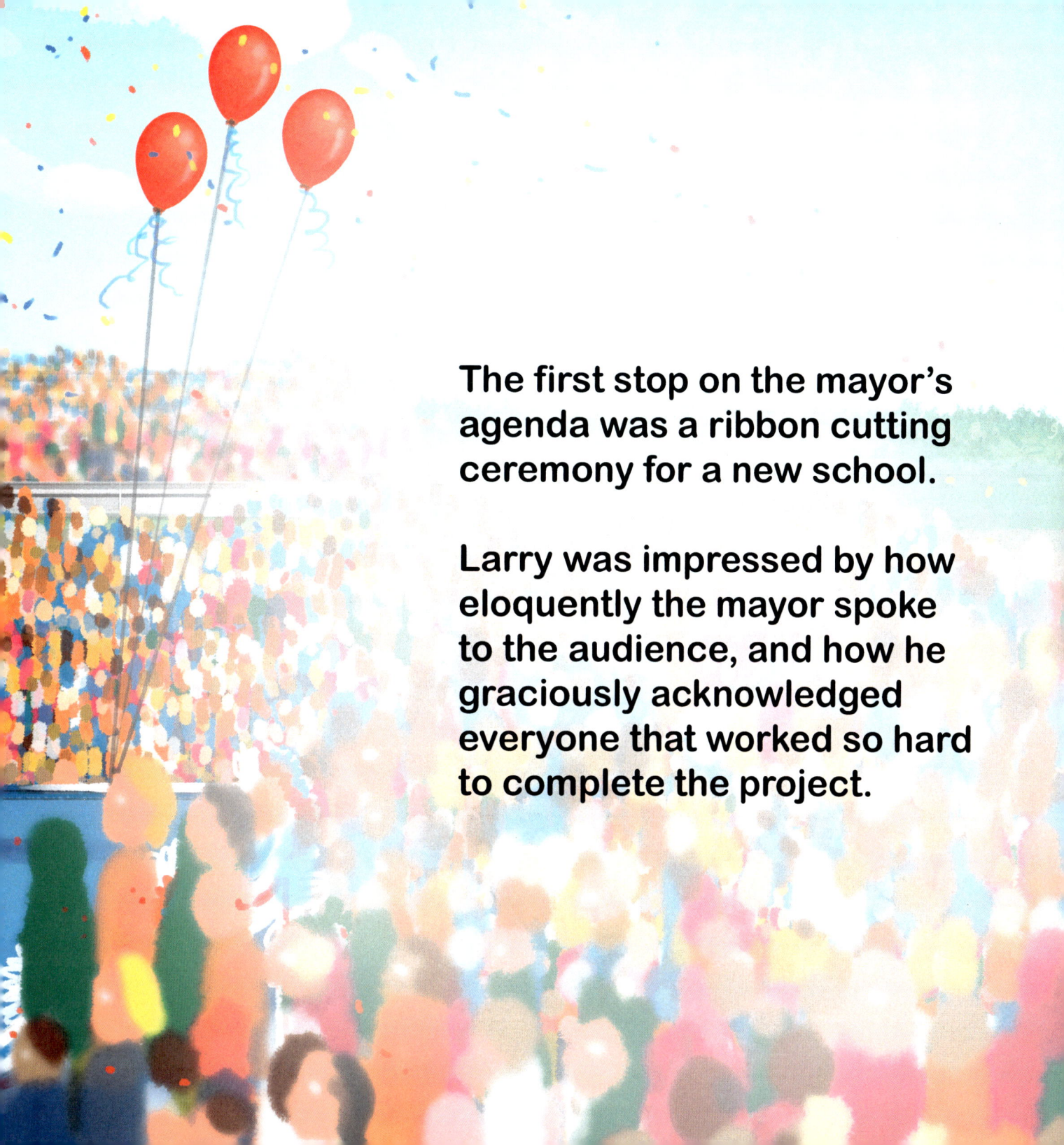

The first stop on the mayor's agenda was a ribbon cutting ceremony for a new school.

Larry was impressed by how eloquently the mayor spoke to the audience, and how he graciously acknowledged everyone that worked so hard to complete the project.

Next, Larry and the mayor attended a groundbreaking ceremony for a new park. Afterward, Larry observed as a businessman attempted to hand Mayor Prince an envelope full of money. Mayor Prince refused to take the money and politely instructed the man to leave.

Larry asked the mayor why he refused the money and asked the man to leave.

"Larry, as a public official, I am not allowed to take money or gifts. The man was seeking a special favor in return for his money.

The citizens who elected me expect me to treat everyone fairly, and that is exactly what I do. Larry, no matter what temptation a man is faced with, he lives by his values and does the right thing, even when no one is watching."

After his day with the mayor, Larry ran to hug his mom.

"Thanks, Mom. Now I know what it means to be a man," he said proudly. He realized that even though he didn't have a father, he had father figures to look up to.

"You're welcome," his mom said, thrilled that her son now understood the qualities that make a good man.

That night Larry's mom looked at him lovingly. "Larry, I know that your father would be so proud of you."

"How do you know that, Mom?"

"Because," she said through a tearful smile, "when you were born, your father buried that metal box in the backyard. He hoped that you would find it one day and learn what qualities a man should have."

THE END

Derrich Phillips is a proud veteran of the United States Army. He is the author of multiple books for children and teenagers, including Poverty Powerball: Turn Adversity Into Your Winning Ticket. Also, his wife is the author of the second book in the Father Figures series, Tina's First Dance. Derrich currently resides in Dallas, Texas with his wife Requill Phillips, daughter Legacy, and "dogter" Empress.

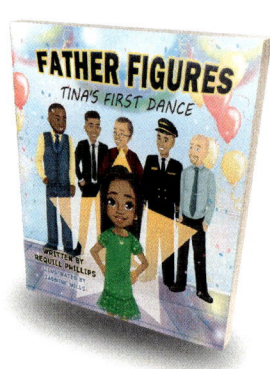

If you enjoyed this book please leave us a review on Amazon and check out the other book in the Father Figures series. Visit www.father-figures.com to claim your exclusive bonus offers.

Made in the USA
Coppell, TX
09 March 2020